First Facts®

Positively Pets

Caring for Your

Snake

by Kathy Feeney

Consultant:
Jennifer Zablotny, DVM
Member, American Veterinary Medical Association

Capstone press®

Mankato, Minnesota

First Facts is published by Capstone Press,
151 Good Counsel Drive, P.O. Box 669, Mankato, Minnesota 56002.
www.capstonepress.com

Library of Congress Cataloging-in-Publication Data
Feeney, Kathy, 1954–
    Caring for your snake/by Kathy Feeney.
    p. cm. — (First facts. Positively pets)
    Summary: "Describes caring for a snake, including supplies needed, feeding, cleaning, health,
safety, and aging" — Provided by publisher.
    Includes bibliographical references and index.
    ISBN-13: 978-1-4296-1257-9 (hardcover)
    ISBN-10: 1-4296-1257-6 (hardcover)
    1. Snakes as pets — Juvenile literature. I. Title. II. Series.
SF459.S5F44 2008
639.3'96 — dc22   2007030371

Editorial Credits

Gillia Olson, editor; Bobbi J. Wyss, set designer; Kyle Grenz, book designer; Sandra D'Antonio,
    illustrator; Kelly Garvin, photo researcher/photo stylist

Photo Credits

All photos Capstone Press/Karon Dubke, except page 20, Getty Images Inc./AFP

Capstone Press thanks Daniel Kladges and Pet Expo, both of Mankato, Minnesota, for assistance
    with photo shoots for this book.

1 2 3 4 5 6 13 12 11 10 09 08

Table of Contents

Do You Want a Snake?

You love their slithering, coiling bodies. They're quiet and don't smell. Plus, there are many pet snake choices. Garter, milk, racer, and rat snakes can make good pets. Even some boas and pythons can be pets. But snakes need a lot of care. Are you ready for this responsibility?

Different types of snakes have different needs. Learn all you can about me so you can give me a good home.

Supplies to Buy

A **terrarium** makes a great snake home. It should have a secure screen top so your snake can't escape.

Other supplies depend on the type of snake. You might need a light to create day and night for the snake. You might need a water spray bottle to get the right **humidity** level. Climbing snakes need branches or ropes.

7

Snakes are **cold-blooded**. They are the same temperature as their surroundings. They change their temperature by moving between hot and cool areas. You can make these areas with a heat lamp and heating pad. Use **thermometers** to check the temperature often.

Your Snake at Home

Let your snake get used to its new home for a few days. Don't make any fast moves near it. Later, you can handle your snake gently.

Keep your pet snake away from other pets. Dogs and cats can hurt or kill a snake. Snakes may want to eat pet hamsters, mice, or even other snakes.

Feeding Your Snake

Snakes are meat eaters. Mice, bugs, and birds are common snake foods. Experts can tell you what food your snake needs and how much to use.

Snakes like to eat alone. Give your snake a covered spot in the terrarium where it can eat. It can also use the covered area to rest.

Cleaning

Snakes don't need baths, but you must clean their homes. Line the floor with paper. You can easily change it. Also make sure the water bowl is clean.

After you hold your snake, wash your hands. Snakes may carry germs called **salmonella.** These germs can make people sick.

Your Snake's Health

The right terrarium conditions help keep your snake healthy. Watch your pet to see how it acts when it's healthy. Signs of sickness include not eating or being less active. If you see a change in your snake, visit a **veterinarian**.

I shed my skin every few months. It's called molting. First, my skin will look dull and my eyes will be cloudy. Soon, I'll crawl right out of my old skin!

Your Snake's Life

Snakes can live from 10 to 25 years. Some keep growing their whole lives. Make sure to check the size of an adult snake before buying a baby.

You and your pet snake will have a long life together. Keeping your snake safe and healthy will make your pet's life a happy one.

Wild Relatives!

More than 2,000 types of snakes crawl around earth. The longest type is the reticulated python. These pythons can eat animals as large as sheep. They have even been known to eat people. The record length for a reticulated python is 32 feet (9.8 meters). But there may be even larger ones out in the wild.

Decode Your Snake's Behavior

- Snakes flick their tongues to smell. Snakes may also flick their tongues when they feel scared.

- Snakes hiss when they sense danger or to scare other animals.

- Snakes rub against things to find out what they are.

- Usually, snakes bite only when they feel they are in danger.

- When they molt, snakes might not move much or eat. They also don't like to be handled.

Glossary

cold-blooded (KOHLD-BLUHD-id) — having a body temperature that changes with the surrounding temperature

humidity (hyoo-MID-uh-tee) — the measure of the moisture in the air

salmonella (sal-muh-NEL-uh) — germs that cause food poisoning and other sicknesses in people; snakes can carry these germs.

terrarium (tuh-RER-ee-uhm) — a glass or plastic container for raising land animals

thermometer (thur-MOM-uh-tur) — a tool that measures temperature

veterinarian (vet-ur-uh-NER-ee-uhn) — a doctor who treats sick or injured animals; veterinarians also help animals stay healthy.

Read More

Craats, Rennay. *Caring for Your Snake.* Caring for Your Pet. New York: Weigl, 2005.

Randolph, Joanne. *Snakes.* Classroom Pets. New York: PowerKids Press, 2007.

Whiting, Jim. *Care for a Pet Snake.* A Robbie Reader. Hockessin, Del.: Mitchell Lane, 2008.

Internet Sites

FactHound offers a safe, fun way to find Internet sites related to this book. All of the sites on FactHound have been researched by our staff.

Here's how:

1. Visit *www.facthound.com*

2. Choose your grade level.

3. Type in this book ID **1429612576** for age-appropriate sites. You may also browse subjects by clicking on letters, or by clicking on pictures and words.

4. Click on the **Fetch It** button.

FactHound will fetch the best sites for you!

Index

3 1524 00493 1285